PUFFIN BOOKS

The Photofit Myste
Jug Valley Juniors

Handles & Spouts, o
to keep an eye on Esme's house. It's up
because her widower father has left for New
Zealand and Esme is now living with her aunty.
But Esme feels protective about the house, and is
sure she sees an intruder in it when she comes by
one afternoon.

That same day Amy notices car headlights
coming from an old barn in the field behind.
They are soon sure they have evidence that
someone is going into the house. But the estate
agents are able to explain everything – everything
except the car headlights. Hands are not to be
put off and are once again hot on the trail in
this fourth spine-tingling adventure about the
friends from Jug Valley Juniors.

Anne Digby was born in Kingston upon Thames,
Surrey, but has lived in the West Country for
many years. As well as the *Jug Valley* books, she
is the author of the popular *Trebizon* and *Me,
Jill Robinson* stories.

The
Photofit Mystery
at Jug Valley Juniors

Anne Digby
Story devised with **Alan Davidson**

Illustrated by
Piers Sanford

PUFFIN BOOKS

PUFFIN BOOKS

Published by the Penguin Group
Penguin Books Ltd, 27 Wrights Lane, London W8 5TZ, England
Penguin Books USA Inc., 375 Hudson Street, New York, New York 10014, USA
Penguin Books Australia Ltd, Ringwood, Victoria, Australia
Penguin Books Canada Ltd, 10 Alcorn Avenue, Toronto, Ontario, Canada M4V 3B2
Penguin Books (NZ) Ltd, 182–190 Wairau Road, Auckland 10, New Zealand

Penguin Books Ltd, Registered Offices: Harmondsworth, Middlesex, England

First published 1992
10 9 8 7 6 5 4 3 2 1

Text copyright © Anne Digby, 1992
Illustrations copyright © Piers Sanford, 1992
All rights reserved

The moral right of the author has been asserted
Filmset in Monophoto Baskerville

Made and printed in Great Britain by
Clays Ltd, St Ives plc

Contents

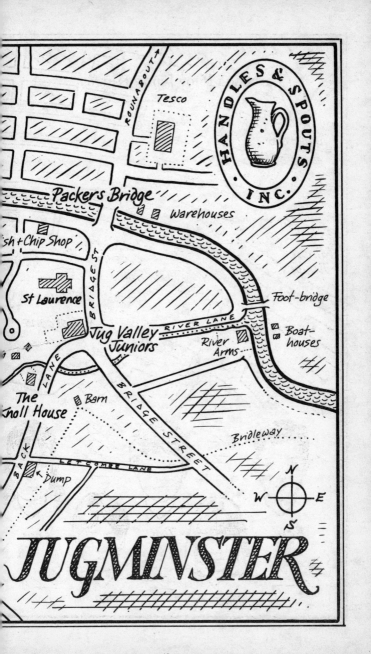

This book is for Jenny Kluga

chapter 1

Esme's Shadow

Esme kept the news to herself for a week. She didn't feel ready to talk about it yet. She certainly didn't want people asking questions. So nobody else in Class 6A knew a thing until she told Handles & Spouts all about it. Hands should have picked it up for themselves. There were one or two clues, after all, and they prided themselves on their powers of observation. But anyway they had plenty of school work to think about that week.

Handles & Spouts Incorporated, Hands for short, consisted of twins Tim and Amy Dalladay; Ben Brown; Ludo Johnson; and Mini Minter – Amy's best friend.

They all liked Esme Kirk. Esme was in their class: a pale, fair girl with spindly legs and a shy, sweet smile. Sometimes if Amy and Mini met Esme coming out of her gate, on to Back Lane, the three girls would walk the last bit to school together. Jug Valley Juniors was at the end of Back Lane, on the corner of Bridge Street.

Esme lived in a peeling little house called The Nook. It snuggled there at the top of its long strip of front garden, well back from the road. A thick hedge along the road frontage meant that only by peering over the gate could the house be glimpsed at all. It had no garage and no back garden. When Amy went to tea there once, she discovered that its small rear yard backed directly on to a farmer's field. She and Esme had run across the field and played in an old barn.

However, the long strip of front garden was densely cultivated, like an allotment. There were rows of carrots, peas, cabbages, tomatoes, lettuces and runner beans. On the way to the front door, beside the garden path, stood a wooden bird-table. Mr Kirk had made it for Esme, who fed the birds every morning.

There was only the two of them.

After Esme's mother had died, Mr Kirk had wondered whether he'd be able to keep paying the mortgage on The Nook on his own. However, he'd managed it

somehow; managed to keep everything
together for them. He was a small,
outwardly cheerful man, who believed in
doing the very best he could by his
daughter.

Handles & Spouts had no idea that
anything had happened.

They knew that Esme was staying with
her aunt this week. They'd seen her arrive
and leave by the school bus, the one that
called at Pelham St Cross, her aunty's
village. But that was nothing unusual.

Mr Kirk was a relief dairyman and self-
employed. If his work took him to a

distant farm, he had to stay away. Then Esme would be parked with his sister in Pelham and be bussed to school for a few days.

Hands had also noticed, even Tim, how quiet and withdrawn Esme seemed this week. Amy and Mini had joined her in the hall one dinner-time, all eating their sandwiches together, but Esme hardly spoke.

'She seemed miles away, didn't she, Mini?' Amy whispered afterwards.

'Wonder if anything's wrong?' replied Mini.

Even when they saw Esme's new clothes, first thing on Thursday morning, they didn't twig. Amy spotted them from right across the playground, as Esme was getting off the bus. She and Mini ran and met Esme coming in through the school gates.

'*Like* your skirt, Esme!' she whispered. '*And* your top. You lucky thing.'

Esme tended to wear very cheap things, although she managed to look nice in them. But this was something different. Amy knew exactly how much the skirt and top cost! They were brand-new stock at Danby's, in Cheap Street. She'd pressed her nose against the window last Saturday, longing for them but knowing that Mum would say they were too expensive.

'Do they look OK?' asked Esme self-consciously.

'Brill!' said Mini approvingly. First bell was ringing. She linked arms with Esme as they all walked into school together. 'Where'd you get them from?'

'Danby's,' replied Esme shyly. 'Aunty Jan helped me choose. She bought them for me.'

'Lucky thing,' repeated Amy.

They were pleased to see her looking so nice. But it was slightly intriguing. Esme's aunt didn't usually buy clothes for her. She had three small children of her own and little money to spare. And it wasn't Esme's birthday or anything.

Then on Friday they discovered the truth.

'Come back, Jax!' laughed Ben. 'Come back at once, you stupid dog!'

After tea on Friday, Tim and Ludo had gone with Ben to take Jax for a walk, while Amy and Mini went up to Bridge Street to buy some crisps. They'd all met up in Back Lane. And now Jax was misbehaving. Nosing round The Nook's

13

garden gate, he'd found it open and charged into the garden, barking.

'Come back, you idiot!' called Ben, pursuing Jax through the gate, followed by the other four, who were all grinning. Ben was always trying to convince himself that Jax was a really well-trained dog!

Woofing happily, Jax bounded along the garden path towards Esme's bird-table. A group of small birds, two sparrows, three blue tits and a wren, were enjoying some crumbs. When Jax appeared below and gazed up at them with a friendly bark, they ignored him and finished their tea.

'Silly fool, Jax,' laughed Tim. He and Ben took the dog by the collar after the birds had flown. 'Come on, let's get him out of here.'

'Put him on the lead, Ben!' suggested Ludo, wandering up with Amy and Mini.

Then a figure suddenly stepped out from behind a row of runner beans.

'Hi, Esme!' exclaimed Amy in surprise. 'You're back home, then?'

'Sorry about this, Es,' muttered Ben, clipping the lead on to Jax's collar.

Esme didn't reply. She just stood there looking pale and trembly and glancing towards the house.

'Sorry!' repeated Ben, seeing her startled face. 'Didn't mean to give you a fright!'

'No. No. It's not that.' Esme shook her head. She stared back towards the house. 'I'm wondering if there's someone upstairs. I thought I saw a shadow flit past that window just now.'

'Must have been your dad,' said Tim helpfully.

Tim's words had an extraordinary effect on Esme. Her shoulders started to heave and funny little croaking sounds came from her throat. Tim's jaw sagged in surprise.

'Are you feeling OK?' asked Ludo anxiously.

Large tears were welling up in her eyes. The croaking sounds were sobs. Worriedly, the five friends gathered round.

'What's wrong, Es?' said Ben.

'Is – is it something to do with your dad?' asked Amy. 'Is he ill or in hospital or something?'

Esme shook her head violently. Quickly she rubbed her eyes with the back of her hand. She turned away from them, to get a grip on herself.

'It's OK. Sorry. I'm being stupid. You don't know, do you? I haven't told

15

anybody yet. It couldn't have been Dad.
He's not in England any more. He's in
New Zealand. He's got a fantastic job out
there. They asked him to come out.'

She turned round and faced them all.
She seemed to have recovered her
composure.

'It's good, isn't it?' she said.

'Will – will he be gone for long?' asked
Ben cautiously.

Esme bit her lip. For the past hour, here
in the garden, she'd been playing a game
of make-believe. She'd saved some of her
packed lunch. She'd been feeding the
birds, a little at a time, then hiding and
watching them. The way she so often did,
while Dad was cooking their supper. But
now she forced herself to say the words, to
say them out loud.

'He's gone to New Zealand for good,'
she stated. 'I don't live in Back Lane any
more. I live with Aunty Jan and Uncle
Roger.'

Handles & Spouts stared at her in shock.

'Dad thinks it's for the best,' Esme was
saying. 'He thinks it'll be much better for
me, with Aunty Jan. He rang me on
Wednesday, from New Zealand!' she
added proudly.

'And what's happening to the house, then?' asked Ludo, the first to recover.

'It's up for sale,' replied Esme. 'With Jermyn's.'

'But there isn't any board,' said Amy, still finding the news hard to digest. She looked at the windows of the little house. 'And all the curtains are still here and everything.'

'And the furniture,' replied Esme. She stared at the ground. 'All our things, Dad's and mine . . . all our furniture and stuff.' She was looking upset again. 'Jermyn's are going to auction the whole lot off, as soon as they've managed to sell the house.'

'And you really thought you saw a shadow?' asked Tim, changing the subject quickly. It'd be embarrassing if Esme started blubbing again. 'Squatters or something?'

'Yes. And nobody's going to squat in *our* house!' said Esme fiercely. 'Nobody's going to touch *our* things. Dad's and mine. Not ever!'

It was such a sudden outburst! The others fell silent, not knowing what to say. Tim thought Esme was being silly. It was up to the estate agents to look after the house now. Seeing that everything was up

for sale anyway, it didn't really have much
to do with her any more! But he was
tactful and kept quiet.

'Let's have a look, then,' said Ben,
kindly. The house seemed all still and
forlorn to him. But just to humour Esme,
he took Jax over to the front door on the
lead and let him sniff around. Then he
came back. 'Nobody there, Es,' he said.
'Else Jax would have started barking.'

'I expect you just imagined seeing a
shadow,' said Ludo, looking wise. Ludo had
read books about things like this. 'You're so
used to there being somebody at home . . .'

'The light must have been playing tricks!' Mini cut in, to shut Ludo up.

Esme nodded and stole a glance at the house, to make sure.

Amy put an arm round her shoulders. Poor Esme!

'Look, you're just torturing yourself,' she said. 'You shouldn't really be coming here, should you?'

At that very moment, like an echo, a voice called from the gate.

'*Esme!* You know you've no business here! Come out of that garden at once! Come along and don't be such a silly girl!'

It was her Aunty Jan.

chapter 2
Mysterious Headlights

*E*sme tore herself away and hurried down the path. Handles & Spouts followed but kept their distance. When they came out into the lane, they saw that Esme's aunt was now talking to her beside a parked car. None of them had heard it arrive.

It was an old Ford car, rusting in places. It was parked alongside The Nook's front hedge. There were three small children in the back seat, their faces pressed to the nearside window.

'I told you to wait at the school!' scolded Aunty Jan. She was a plump woman with a friendly face but right now she was looking tired and cross. 'I told you when

you phoned that I couldn't come till Uncle
Roger got back with the car! Whatever
made you miss the bus? You should have
waited for me up at school, like I told
you.'

Handles & Spouts hung back by the
gate, trying to look invisible.

'I was just coming, Aunty,' said Esme,
looking shamefaced. 'I didn't mean to
frighten you –'

'Whatever are you doing here?' repeated
her aunt.

'I was worried about the birds. I
thought . . .'

As Esme's voice trailed away, her aunt
looked upset. She gave Tim and Amy &
Co. the briefest of glances then shepherded
Esme towards the passenger door.

'Now, say goodbye to your friends.
Promise me you'll never do this again,
Essy! You just forget about The Nook. It's
nothing to do with you! It's not your home
any more, my love. Your home's with *us*
now. Uncle Roger got that little TV set
for you today! He's put it in your room.
Your dad's gone to start his new life and
you've got to start yours! Daddy has
money to spare now. And just think, when
The Nook's been sold . . . all the nice

things he wants us to buy you! And
another thing – '

Aunty Jan was opening the car door for
Esme. Esme was getting in, very slowly,
like a film in slow motion. Not smiling.
Just gazing helplessly towards her front
gate and the five of them standing there,
frozen. And Aunty Jan was saying, '– he
promised to ring you up again tonight,
didn't he? He'll tell you some more about
New Zealand! There, that's something to
look forward to!'

The door slammed.

Aunty Jan looked harassed behind the
driving wheel as she nosed along Back
Lane, looking for a turning place. Handles
& Spouts waited by The Nook's gate and
watched the car turn.

As it came back, they all waved
goodbye. But Esme didn't wave back. She
seemed to be speaking urgently to her
aunt. The car had just passed them when
they heard the squeal of brakes. They
looked round and saw Esme leap out.

She came running back to them, along
the lane.

'It's all right,' she whispered, panting
for breath slightly. She glanced back over
her shoulder. 'I've pretended to Aunty

22

that I've forgotten to pay you some money back.'

They all gathered round. Esme kept her voice low.

'It's about your secret club, you do things and stuff, don't you?'

'That's right,' said Tim, chest puffing out.

'Could you keep a look-out this weekend?' she begged. 'I mean, I don't want you to go to any special trouble or anything. But if you see anything funny could you go and report it to Jermyn's? They're open all weekend. Or tell me at school on Monday. I mean, I know it's stupid, but I think there might be some squatters. And it *is* still our house, isn't it? Dad's and mine. Till it gets sold, anyway.'

They all nodded.

'Be pleased to help,' said Tim handsomely.

Just up the lane, the car honked. Aunty Jan was in a hurry to get back to Pelham. The little ones were hungry. And what if John's call came through from New Zealand before they got back? Roger would tell him about Esme missing the bus! He'd get all worked up and worried and feel helpless on the other side of the world. It was bad enough already, Esme bursting into tears when he'd phoned her on Wednesday . . .

'What makes you so sure, Esme?' asked Ludo with interest.

'I'm not a *bit* sure. It was just a funny feeling. Apart from the shadow, I sort of felt a presence, people there who shouldn't be. I expect I *did* imagine things. But if there were people in our house, I just couldn't bear it. Not in my room and everything, touching my furniture! Messing everything up. I need to feel safe and secure and know everything's fine, just as we left it. Dad and I.'

The car honked again. She gazed at them imploringly.

'Leave it to us, Es!' said Ben quickly.

'It's all in hand!' said Tim enthusiastically.

'So don't *worry*,' smiled Amy, touching Esme's arm.

'You'd better run!' added Mini.

Esme raced off to the car. Before getting in, she turned back and waved.

'Thanks again!' she shouted. She looked relieved.

'See you on Monday!' they called back.

As the car drove off, they went into a huddle. They all agreed to keep an eye on

24

The Nook, over the weekend. A promise
was a promise. But they were just
humouring Esme, really. They didn't think
there was anyone in the house.

'She just feels protective about it, doesn't
she?' mused Amy. 'She can't face up to
the idea of other people living there.'

'She's going to have to, soon,' said Tim,
practically.

'That was part of her packed lunch that
she was feeding the birds with,'
commented the sharp-eyed Ludo. 'She
must have planned to come. She must
have missed the bus deliberately!'

It was starting to drizzle with rain. They put their collars up and turned for home. Jax was straining at the leash.

'The funny thing is,' Mini confided to Amy as they trailed behind, eating their crisps, 'she used to grumble about the house sometimes. She told me it was poky and they didn't have any nice furniture!'

Amy thought about it. She grumbled about *their* house sometimes. The Knoll House always had things wrong with it.

'That's different,' she pointed out. She sighed. 'Anyway, it won't be just the house and furniture she's missing.'

One of the things wrong with the Knoll House was the central-heating system. It was very old and didn't work. Mr and Mrs Dalladay hoped to replace it, one day.

Amy's attic bedroom, like Tim's, got chilly at nights. Every evening at dusk Amy would run upstairs and draw her curtains. They were extremely thick and definitely helped to keep the warmth in.

She went upstairs on Friday night, passing Harry's bedroom on the way. The door was open. Their baby brother was sitting up in his cot, noisily pretending to

26

read a book out loud. He never went to
sleep when he was supposed to.

'I'll pop down and hear you read in a
minute, Harry,' laughed Amy, stopping
by. 'And then you promise to go to sleep!'

She continued up to the attic floor.
Tim's bedroom door was open and he was
practising walking on his hands. It was
gym club in the morning.

Amy went into her room and stared out
of the window. She had a great view from
up here. She could see the lights on in
Mini's house, number 27, opposite. Other
lights, too, coming on in houses further
along Back Lane. She started to think
about Esme Kirk. She craned her neck to
see if she could glimpse The Nook. But it
was out of sight, just round the bend.

She couldn't actually see The Nook, yet
through a gap between roof-tops she could
see part of the field behind. There was
darkness descending over it. She could just
make out the shadowy hulk of a distant
building. It was the old barn. The one
that stood across the field at the back of
The Nook, where she and Esme had
messed around that time. She hadn't
realized you could see it from here.

Poor Esme, she thought, having to start

27

a new life. She'd always got on so well
with her dad. In spite of the new clothes
and the TV set and the fact that Aunty
Jan and Uncle Roger were very kind,
maybe she preferred the old life! That must
be why she hadn't told anyone. She'd been
trying to cling on to it a little bit longer.
She still was! If Ludo was right, she'd
deliberately missed the school bus this
afternoon to go to The Nook.

That apart, thought Amy, standing
there in her own bedroom, it *was* special,
wasn't it? A place that had once been your
home. Even if it was a bit grotty. It was a
chunk of your life. It was part of you,
really.

Well, Esme mustn't worry! They'd be
her eyes and ears. While The Nook was
forlorn and unoccupied, they'd watch it
for her, protect it. Maybe Amy would feed
the birds tomorrow.

She started to draw the curtains across.
Then she took a quick breath.

There were two pinpricks of light
emerging from the distant barn.

'Tim!' she called. 'Here, quick! I've just
seen something mysterious.'

Her twin brother came wobbling across
the landing on his hands. He entered the

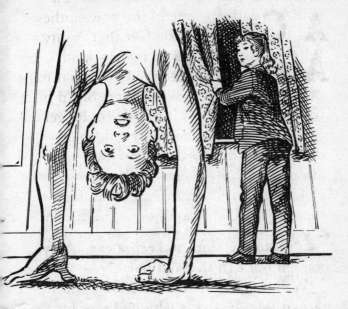

room, still walking on his hands, legs
waving in the air.

'Where?'

'Stand up the right way, you idiot.
Come and have a look!'

They pressed their faces against the
window. Amy pointed.

The pinpricks of light stabbed into the
gloaming as they left the barn. They
headed towards some trees, briefly
illuminating them. Then they disappeared
behind them into a more distant field.

'Car headlights,' said Tim. 'What of it?'

chapter 3
A Case,
After All

'It's a funny place to keep a car,' Amy pointed out. 'In that old barn.'

'Well, maybe the farmer hasn't got a garage. Maybe that's why he keeps his car there!' replied Tim.

'What, miles away from the farmhouse?' frowned Amy. 'The only place that barn's anywhere near is The Nook.'

'The Nook?' Tim's ears pricked up.

'Yes. That's what I mean. The field that barn stands in runs behind The Nook! The barn's got double doors and it's full of old junk and stuff. Esme took me in there once. Nobody keeps a car in there. I mean, not usually. It's not even got a road to it! Just a bumpy track that leads into the next field. Don't know where it goes after that.'

'It must have been a tractor, then. With its lights on.'

'Why would a tractor go out at night?' asked Amy.

'Dunno.' Tim peered through the window, beginning to feel quite interested. 'It's gone off over the next field, hasn't it? No sign of it now.'

'Maybe there *are* some squatters or hippies or something and they've got a car!' whispered Amy. She drew the curtains. 'They'd have to hide it during the day. The barn'd be a good place.'

'*If* there are some,' said Tim.

All the same, he was curious.

While Amy was busy with Harry, he dashed down to the kitchen and got the big torch. It was hanging on a hook by the back door.

'Going somewhere, Tim?' asked Mrs Dalladay sharply, looking up from her book. She was sitting by the Aga, warming her toes, waiting for the bread to bake. It smelt good. 'It's dark.'

'Just nipping outside, Mum,' Tim mumbled. 'Won't be a sec.'

He crossed Back Lane and ran towards The Nook, shining the torch ahead of him.

He reached its little front gate and looked over, down the long garden path. He could just glimpse the house.

He blinked. Was he imagining it?

Crikey, he thought. There's a light on upstairs.

Looking at that dim glow in the upper right-hand window, his scalp prickled.

He turned and ran for home, his heart bumping.

It looked, Tim decided, as though Handles & Spouts had a case on their hands, after all.

After activities the next morning, they went straight to The Nook, all five of them. Safety in numbers, they agreed.

They always went to JVJ on a Saturday morning. They all belonged to gym club, except Ludo, who belonged to chess club. Otherwise they'd have gone to investigate sooner.

Hands stopped by the garden gate, cautiously. It would be embarrassing if Mr Jermyn, the estate agent, were showing anybody over the house! But everything appeared deserted.

'All clear,' said Ben.

Then a quick glance up and down Back

Lane, to make sure there was no one around . . .

'OK,' said Tim.

He clicked open the gate and they all sidled through.

They moved softly through the front garden, up towards the house. It was exciting but a little scary, too.

'Which window did you see the light in, Tim?' whispered Ludo.

'That one,' replied Tim, pointing.

Ludo pulled up. He cupped his hands round his eyes, gazing towards the upper right window. 'Wait!' he said.

'What?' asked Amy.

'I think it's still on. You can't really tell in daylight. Unless you do this –'

They all followed suit and cupped their hands round their eyes.

'Yes,' said Mini. 'You could be right, Lu. But it's a very dim one.'

'It was last night,' said Tim.

'Maybe it's been on all the time?' suggested Ludo. 'Maybe the agents just leave it on. People do that sometimes, to scare off burglars.'

'What about the car headlights, then?' asked Tim, looking nettled. 'How d'you explain those?'

33

'Yes, come on,' said Ben. 'Let's have a good scout round if we're going to.'

'I was only making an observation,' said Ludo.

They tiptoed off in different directions. Tim bent down by the front door and peeped through the letter-box. There was just a tiny hall with some stairs leading straight up. Amy and Mini peered through a window into the sitting-room. It was very tidy. It didn't look as though anybody had used it lately.

Then Ben's face appeared round the corner of the house. He looked excited.

'Round the back!' he hissed. 'Come and look at this.'

They followed Ben round into the little back yard. It was just as Amy remembered it. She stole a glance at the huge field behind, covered in stubble, with the old barn on the far side. Even from this distance she could see that its big double doors were firmly shut. Tim snatched a quick look, too. But it was the house that interested Ben. He made straight for the kitchen windows.

'Look!' he repeated.

Handles & Spouts pressed their noses against the glass, though Mini had to

stand on an upturned bucket to get a good
view.

A surprising sight greeted them.

'So there *are* people using the house!'
gasped Tim.

The kitchen table was covered in a cloth
and laid for tea. Three places had been
laid. There were three plates and three
knives and three cups and saucers. A tub
of margarine stood in the centre of the
table and next to it a jar of strawberry
jam, half full. On the draining-board were
some upturned breakfast bowls which could
have been left there from the morning.

'They're out for lunch, then,' observed Ludo drily. 'The table's laid for tea.'

'Come on,' whispered Ben. 'Let's get out of here!'

They ran as fast as they could up the front garden, then out through the gate. They leaned into the hedge on Back Lane, puffing and panting.

'What do we do now?' asked Mini, feeling rather excited.

'Go to Jermyn's, of course!' said Tim. 'Come on. We've got time before lunch, if we hurry.'

'OK!' agreed Ben. 'Action! What are we waiting for?'

They set off at a jog for the centre of town.

chapter **4**
At Jermyn's

*I*t was quite a trot to Jermyn's. It was
on the other side of the Jug, nearly
opposite Jugminster Abbey. This area was
the heart of the old town. Many of the
buildings were listed as being of historic
interest, including Jermyn's. The hanging
out of garish signs was forbidden. The
windows were old-fashioned leaded, not
plate glass. So the estate agency had a
very dignified appearance. A small card in
the window whispered, in copperplate
handwriting: *Jermyn & Sons are pleased to
announce that they are now open seven days a
week.*

Once over Abbey Bridge, the friends had
slowed to a walk. Now they peered at the
colour photographs in the windows, while
getting their breath back and screwing up
the courage to go inside. It was a daunting

place. The photos of houses had spotlights shining on them, to show them off.

'Can't see The Nook in the window,' said Tim.

'It's not posh enough, is it?' said Ben. 'Come on, let's go in and get it over with. They'll be pleased we've come when we tell them.'

'Hope you're right,' muttered Ludo uneasily. 'Hope we haven't leapt to the wrong conclusions.'

'Don't be chicken, Lu!' said Ben crossly, and they bundled Ludo up amongst them as they shoved through the door.

The bell jangled horribly.

It was dim and hushed inside, with thick pile carpet.

They were in the big front office of Jermyn's. It went back a long way and seemed to be quietly humming with activity. Customers were sitting at little tables and being shown folders. They seemed to be whispering about mortgages and things.

At the first desk, just inside the door, a woman was saying, 'Delightful little riverside cottages like these don't often come up, madam,' to a lady in a big hat.

The hushed voices made Tim think of a hospital.

'Yes?' asked the woman at the near desk, loudly. She was very well groomed. The name-plate on her desk said, RECEPTION – MS DEE FENDER. Her disdainful look made it clear that she didn't consider them important customers. They became aware, especially the Spouts, that they looked a mess. The whole of the front office had gone silent and heads were turning their way. At the back, the door of Mr Jermyn's private office opened. He peered out of his inner sanctum to see what was happening.

Amy smoothed down her track-suit top and wished they'd had a chance to tidy up before they came.

'Yes?' repeated Ms Fender impatiently. The lady in the big hat was staring at them.

'We want to see the manager, please,' Mini piped up, pointing to the back office.

'I'm afraid Mr Jermyn's very busy at the moment,' replied Ms Fender with icy sweetness. 'He's got a client with him –'

'No, he hasn't!' said Ben loudly.

'I'm afraid he only sees people by appointment. If you'd like to tell me what it's about –' she said snappily.

'It's private,' said Mini. 'Something important!'

The phone rang and the woman picked it up. 'Jermyn & Sons, Dee Fender speaking.'

'Would you like to come through?' called Mr Jermyn. He'd sized up the situation at a glance and decided that the sooner these scruffy young visitors were swept into the back office the better!

Gratified, Handles & Spouts tramped the length of the front office and crowded round his doorway.

'Do come in,' he said with a nervous smile. 'Come in and sit down.'

He closed the door of the inner sanctum firmly behind them.

'Now, what can I do for you?'

'Please, sir, we think there are some squatters in one of the houses you're trying to sell!' Mini blurted out.

He looked interested at first but then, as they explained, he began to yawn and look at his watch. It was rather unnerving.

'Oh, The Nook, eh?' he interrupted. 'And you're friends of Mr Kirk's daughter. Well, it's none of your business, but I'll let you into a secret.'

To their dismay, he seemed to be laughing at them.

'Those were Mr Kirk's own instructions!

To leave the light on and the table laid and so forth. Gone to work in New Zealand. Doesn't want the place vandalized. Got to make it look lived in! So now you know!'

With the exception of Ludo, they all went very red in the face. Ludo just nodded in agreement and looked slightly smug.

'Sorry we disturbed you, sir,' mumbled Tim, feeling a complete fool.

'We'll be on our way, then,' said Ben, getting to his feet.

They all rose. They were longing to escape now. But Mr Jermyn hadn't quite finished with them. He strode across the room and tapped a huge gun-metal grey safe, set in the wall.

'See this safe? Before he went abroad, Mr Kirk had all new locks fitted at The Nook. Doors, windows, everything! The keys are in here. The Nook's the most secure place in Jugminster! *Nobody* can get in. Nobody except us. Satisfied? Good of you to come but you can go away and forget about it now. And, of course, if you don't mind my saying so, you were trespassing. Mustn't do that again, eh?'

He led them to a side door.

'Care to slip out this way? Then we won't disturb the customers. Weekends are our best time, y'know.'

They found themselves ignominiously in the side street, the door closed quietly behind them.

'I thought it was a bit funny, the table being laid for tea!' protested Ludo. 'I mean, who'd bother to do that, when it's still morning?'

'All right! All right!' replied Tim, who felt like hitting him. 'Maybe we should have discussed it more! Maybe we were a bit hasty!'

'I've never felt such an idiot in my whole life,' groaned Ben.

'So much for Esme's shadow,' sniffed Mini. 'We were only doing it for her.'

And they tramped home in silence.

'Well, at least Esme will be pleased,' Amy said to Tim that evening, as he reappeared at the kitchen door. He'd been upstairs to get his sweater and she'd asked him to draw her curtains.

She was toasting her hands by the Aga. It was chilly outside and starting to get dark. This was when she loved to be indoors, in the warmth of the kitchen, with one of Mum's Saturday-night curries on the go and smelling delicious. It had made her think of Esme again. Poor thing, not being in her own little house any more.

But at least she could stop worrying about The Nook; intruders getting in and all that stuff. What a pity that her father hadn't explained to her! He'd taken all those precautions before he left but hadn't bothered to tell Esme. Dads were like that, they didn't always tell you things.

Well, they'd see Esme at school on Monday and make a *full report*. They'd repeat everything Mr Jermyn had told them, word for word. He'd said The Nook was just about the most secure place in Jugminster and, as a professional estate agent, he surely knew what he was talking about!

'We'll be able to put her mind at rest, Tim,' continued Amy. 'So – the Esme mystery. It wasn't a complete waste of time, was it?'

She looked at Tim. He was still standing in the doorway, gazing into space. He hadn't been listening to a word!

'What's wrong with *you*?'

'I've just seen those mysterious headlights again,' said Tim quietly. 'When I was drawing your curtains.'

'What, leaving the barn?' asked Amy. She glanced at the fallen dusk outside. 'But it's the same time again. The same as last night. How weird.'

'I know. That's what I think,' said Tim. He walked over to the Aga and stood next to Amy. They warmed their hands together. 'In fact the whole thing's weird. Now I've seen the barn, I get what you mean about it being a funny place to keep a car. It's in the middle of nowhere! And why does it only go out when it gets dark?'

'But it can't be anything to do with The Nook, can it? We know that now,' said Amy.

'Obviously not,' agreed Tim. 'But it's definitely a mystery. Probably a much better one than the Esme one! D'you think Hands ought to investigate?'

They looked at each other excitedly. After their recent humiliation, they badly needed a success.

'Yes, I *do*!' said Amy. 'Let's have a proper meeting. Let's call one for tomorrow morning!'

Handles & Spouts were back in business.

chapter 5

Ben Stops in his Tracks

*T*hey met at ten o'clock on Sunday morning. Tim brought a map with him to their secret HQ, the old caravan in the orchard.

H & S put their badges on. Mini always claimed that they brought them luck and helped them to think! This morning, the mugs of tea and some chocolate biscuits helped, too.

Everybody was in a good mood again today. The other three had been extremely interested to learn that the headlights had appeared again last night. They agreed with the twins that this mystery held promise; unlike the Esme one, which they wanted to expunge from memory.

'Yes, it's odd,' agreed Ludo. He, too, had noticed the barn yesterday morning and realized it must be the one the twins had mentioned. 'A car that's kept in a lonely barn and only goes out when it's dark.'

'Perhaps it's stolen,' suggested Ben.

'Hidden in the barn during the day,' mused Mini. 'Will it be there now? Let's go and take a look at it! How do we get there?'

'Easy!' laughed Tim. He spread the local ordnance survey map out on the table. It was Dad's, borrowed after breakfast.

'Not thinking of cutting through The Nook, are you?' asked Ludo edgily.

'Bit chancy,' agreed Ben.

Mr Jermyn's heavy warning about trespassing was still ringing in their ears.

'What d'you think I've brought the map for?' retorted Tim. 'There's no need to go that way!'

'We can if we want to!' said Mini pugnaciously. 'Mr Jermyn's a silly old fool. We weren't trespassing. We'd got Esme's permission –'

'It's all right, Mini,' Amy cut in. She and Tim had already had a good look at Dad's map. 'Better steer clear of The

Nook. Look – there's a track. It goes right
past the far side of the barn. And it's a
public right of way.'

They all crowded round the map.

'A bridle-way!' nodded Ludo. 'Good.'

'It crosses Letcombe Lane, see,' said
Tim, pointing. 'We can join it there. We
can double back over the fields and
then –' he stabbed with his finger.
'There's the barn!'

'Bit of a slog, isn't it?' grumbled Mini.

'Going that way. What a long way round!'

Letcombe Lane was a left-hand turning off Back Lane, out in the open countryside.

'Oh, come on, Mini,' laughed Amy. She looked through the caravan window. It was quite bright outside. 'It'll be a nice walk.'

Mini knew that she was outnumbered.

'OK, then! It's just that I'm *dying* to get a look at that car,' she confessed.

They all were. They washed up the tea mugs and left them on the little draining-board. Then they unpinned their badges and put them away in the drawer.

'Can we keep the map a bit longer, Dad?' asked Tim as the five of them trailed up towards the house. His father was attacking the weeds in the vegetable garden. There was couch grass wrapped round his big garden fork. The Knoll House soil grew weeds bigger and tougher and more deep-seated than anybody else's.

'Going for a walk?' asked Mr Dalladay.

Harry, sitting with a trowel in the middle of the garden path, looked up. He'd been frowning in concentration, trying to dig out a dandelion that was rooted in a crack in the path. He'd been

working at it for some time but had only
succeeded in chopping its head off. Now
he jumped up and threw the trowel away
with a loud clatter.

'Walk! Me come!' screamed Harry
excitedly.

He came and flung his arms round
Amy's legs and gazed up at her.

'Please, Mamie!'

Handles & Spouts exchanged wry
glances, then nodded.

'All right, Harry.' Amy ruffled his curly
brown hair.

'Run and get your push-chair, then!'
laughed Tim.

'Going far?' called Mum, looking
pleased. She was leaning out of her studio
window upstairs, watching them leave with
Harry strapped in his push-chair. 'Don't
be late back for Sunday dinner. It's roast
beef and Yorkshire pud! Followed by ice-
cream!'

They regretted taking Harry. It slowed
them up. The little boy begged to be
wheeled round the dump, on the corner of
Letcombe Lane. It took an age to reach
the bridle-way. By this time, Harry was
getting restless and making various

demands: to be let out of the push-chair; to go home; to be given a drink of orange; to have a piggyback; to have some Yorkshire pudding and/or ice-cream.

'We can let him walk a bit now,' said Ben, once they were on the bridle-way. He'd had a long turn of pushing him. He bent down and released the strap.

But Harry wouldn't walk straight. He zigzagged back and forth, finding exciting things that he wanted to take home. They let him keep the acorns and the snail but made him throw away the horse's dropping.

'*Dirty!*' scolded Amy, strapping him back in the push-chair.

'For Daddy!' protested Harry, thinking of the garden.

He was generally cross and grizzly after that, as they wheeled and bumped the push-chair along the uneven track. 'Ollenge!' he whined. And then, every so often, 'Porkshire pud and ice-cream!'

Both were particular passions of his.

'Sorry, little bruv,' said Tim firmly, as they strode along. 'We can't take you home yet. This is an important investigation.'

Soon they all began to feel excited. They knew from the map that the barn was only a couple of fields away now. They'd approach it from the far side.

'This is the way the headlights come then, isn't it?' said Amy eagerly. 'The car leaves the barn and heads along this bridle-way, following the route we've just come till it gets on to a proper road at Letcombe Lane.'

'And it's certainly up to no good,' nodded Ludo. 'Cars aren't allowed here! And who'd want to keep one miles from the road, anyway –'

'Unless they've got a good reason to hide it!' agreed Mini.

'Look!' exclaimed Tim, as they came over the top of a rise. 'There it is!'

The barn was only the length of a field away, in the corner of the adjoining field. From here, it was half hidden behind the line of trees just ahead of them. The trees that the twins had seen so mysteriously illuminated by headlights.

They quickened their pace, hearts thudding. Ben took the push-chair from Amy. He could see that her arms were starting to ache a bit.

'Thanks, Ben,' said Amy, meeting his eyes gratefully. 'Sorry about bruv.'

'No. It's good we've got Harry!' smiled Ben. They were getting ever closer to the

barn. 'If anyone sees us they'll never
suspect we're spies.'

'I never thought of that, Ben!' laughed
Tim. He patted Harry's head as the push-
chair drew abreast. 'Good old Harry.
You're our cover. We're taking our baby
brother out for a Sunday morning walk.'

'Not baby!' Harry pointed out. But he
looked pleased for a while.

The line of trees on their left became a
tall, ragged hedge. They moved cautiously
now, keeping their heads ducked down.

53

Then they halted as they reached a wide gap in the hedge. It led into the next field.

And there, only a few metres away, was the barn. A short length of track ran from its double doors, through the gap in the hedge, to meet up with the bridle-way here.

'This is the way it comes at night, all right,' whispered Tim, nodding in satisfaction.

The timber building's big double doors were closed. They met in the middle and were held shut by two heavy latches.

The five knelt down behind the hedge now, keeping still. With fingers to lips, they listened and watched for the slightest sound or movement. Harry also put his fingers to his lips and kept quiet.

All was still. They could hear some crows cawing in the trees behind them. And the distant droning of a car along Back Lane. Otherwise, nothing.

'All clear,' whispered Mini.

'Come on, then. Into action!' said Ben.

It was agreed that Amy and Ludo should stay with Harry, back towards the trees.

Tim, Ben and Mini tiptoed towards the

barn doors. They peeped all about them, carefully. They were visible in the field now, the big one at the back of The Nook. But there was nobody around. Mini glanced across to The Nook. She could just glimpse its chimney-stack above two small oak trees that grew behind it.

'Quick, inside!' hissed Ben. He lifted the two latches. The three of them quietly eased back the nearest door to make an opening. Then they stepped into the barn, ready to turn tail and flee if anyone challenged them.

Even in the darkness, they saw it was empty – except for the car.

'*Here it is!*' gasped Tim. 'It's almost brand-new!'

They stared at the gleaming black saloon car. It looked quite out of place. It was surrounded by rotting hay-bales, empty oil drums, worn-out tractor tyres and other junk. It was not much used, the barn. Not normally. But it was being used now!

They walked all round the shiny black car, investigating it.

'Doors are locked,' said Tim.

'Come and see what's on the back!' Mini called softly.

She pointed to a little sticker in the rear window:

CONRAD'S CAR HIRE
LONDON

'OK,' nodded Tim. He jerked his head towards the door. 'Let's go.'

They slipped out of the barn as silently as they'd entered, dropping the latches home again. But it was quite safe. There was still no one around.

They raced back to Harry's push-chair. Ludo was sitting cross-legged in front of him, touching the tip of his nose with his tongue. Harry was trying to copy him, while Amy had been keeping anxious watch on the gap in the hedge.

'Well?' she exclaimed, as they came running.

'A brand-new hire-car. A black one!' puffed Mini.

'From London!' panted Ben.

'We're definitely on to something,' added Tim, feeling triumphant.

Ludo's eyes gleamed with interest.

'Probably stolen!' he said. 'Maybe they go out in it at night and rob big country houses.'

56

'D'you think we ought to go and tell the farmer this afternoon?' asked Ben.

'Let's have another meeting first,' said Ludo cautiously. 'Think of all possible angles.'

They pondered. Ludo was right. They didn't want to make fools of themselves again.

'OK,' Tim rapped out. 'Let's get Harry back now. It's getting late! We can all have our dinners, then meet at HQ at two-thirty.'

The words 'Harry' and 'dinner' were too much for the little boy. He suddenly let out a loud wail.

'Porkshire pud!' he screamed. 'Ice-cream!'

'You certainly do, Harry!' groaned Tim. 'Do please stop it.'

But he wouldn't.

Hands looked at one another, all with the same idea. Mini peered through the hedge. Across the next field, tantalizingly close, was that glimpse of The Nook's chimney-pots.

It was all clear, wasn't it? Nobody would see them!

'Oh, come *on*!' laughed Mini. 'We can't go back the way we've come. It's miles.

Not now. Poor Harry, he must be really starving.'

They all agreed with Mini that this was an emergency.

After all, Harry wasn't the only one.

A low wire fence separated the farmer's field from the backyard of The Nook. It was only some old chicken-wire, trodden down in places. The boys lifted Harry's push-chair over it with ease. Then they all scooted round the outside of the house, Tim leading the way with Harry who was feeling cheerful again.

Ben brought up the rear. Being so tall, he gave the merest glance through the kitchen window as he passed.

He stopped dead in his tracks.

'Hey! That's funny!' he called softly.

'What's funny, Ben?' asked Amy, who was just ahead of him.

'The jam pot,' said Ben. 'It's moved.'

chapter 6

HQ is Buzzing

'**H**ow d'you mean, moved?' asked Amy. She called the others back. They all crowded round the kitchen window with Ben. Mini dragged the old bucket over again, not to miss out. But everything looked much the same as yesterday morning. Three places laid for tea at the kitchen table, the breakfast bowls still upturned on the draining-board, behind.

'You sure it's moved, Ben?' asked Ludo, frowning. 'It's next to the margarine tub, where it was yesterday.'

'Except it's facing the other way!' whispered Ben. 'I noticed the label yesterday. *Strawberry jam*, my favourite. But, look! What jam is it? You can't read the label today. That's because the jar's been turned round. The side with the label on's *facing the wall* now!'

59

They drew in their breaths. Ben was right.

'Brill,' said Amy admiringly.

'There's something else . . .' began Mini slowly. She screwed her eyes up tight. Mini had a photographic memory, but first she had to concentrate, hard. 'Yes! I'm positive. I can picture it. The jar was half full.' She opened them again. 'But it's not now! It's only a quarter full, look. Someone's eaten some!'

'Eaten a lot, if you're right, Mini,' said Ben. 'A quarter of a jar!'

'Storeberry jam!' Harry piped up from the push-chair, straining at his straps. 'Let me see!'

'Sh, Harry!' whispered Amy. 'Come on,' she said to the others, 'don't let's hang around!'

She thought of Esme's shadow and gave a little shiver. Even Ludo was taken aback. As they wheeled Harry round to the front of the house, Ludo said, 'Doesn't make sense, does it? Suggest we all keep our eyes skinned as we go up the path. Look for more clues. What about the vegetables?'

Clever Ludo.

Half-way along the front path, Mini fell to her knees.

'Look!' she hissed excitedly. 'This row of carrots!'

They crowded round. Some of the carrots were missing from the row. They'd been dug up, very recently. There was fresh earth scattered around.

Ben glanced back at the house, looking for any sign of movement. Was it possible there *were* people in The Nook, after all?

'Let's run now,' Amy was saying. 'I think we ought to run –'

'Wait,' said Tim. Ben's glancing back had made him do the same. And now he was cupping his hands round his eyes and staring at the left-hand bedroom window. 'It's a different light on today! It's the left-hand one!'

'You're right, Tim!' exclaimed Ludo, shading his eyes to look.

After that, they couldn't get out of the gate fast enough for the safety of Back Lane. There was so much to discuss but there wasn't time now. They'd all be late home for their dinner! A lot of careful thinking was required. It was all very peculiar but they didn't want to make fools of themselves again.

'We'll have to decide what to do, won't we?' said Tim, as they all split up. 'See you at the meeting, OK? Amy and I'll bring the phone down. Just in case we need it.'

'Can I have some more, Mum?' asked Tim.

'Never known you two so hungry!' laughed Mrs Dalladay. 'Nor you, Harry.'

She was cutting Harry's Yorkshire pudding into squares for him. His second helping. There was a blissful expression on his clean, scrubbed face.

'Oi, leave me some roast potatoes, Tim,' smiled Dad.

'That was a lovely long walk!' said Mum later.

'Seems to have exhausted you,' commented Dad. 'You're very quiet.'

'Just thinking, Dad,' said Tim.

'Just thinking how nice Sunday dinner is!' Amy added quickly. 'Delicious, Mum.'

It *was* a nice dinner, Amy thought. Home was nice, too. That's why she'd been thinking about Esme again. She'd been thinking how horrible it would be to come into the garden of the Knoll House and look across to the windows and wonder if someone was in here, touching their things. The way Esme had wondered at The Nook on Friday afternoon. And thinking that she still hadn't been to feed Esme's birds.

At first, they'd only been humouring

Esme. Then, trying to help her, they'd been made to look stupid at Jermyn's. But was it possible, however mad it seemed, that Esme had been right all along?

Later, at the kitchen window, their parents saw the twins walking down the garden, in the direction of the caravan. Mini had just come by, as well. Tim was carrying the radio phone, and Amy, the local phone book.

'HQ seems to be buzzing today,' remarked Mum.

'I wonder what they're up to?' replied Dad.

'Storeberry jam!' explained Harry sleepily. He was lying on a rug on the floor.

Mrs Dalladay laughed and lifted him up.

'Strawberry jam? After all the ice-cream you've eaten? Certainly not. Come on, you silly boy. Upstairs for your nap. Before you zonk out on the kitchen floor!'

'Think we ought to ring Jermyn's, then?' asked Ludo, looking at the phone. The meeting had begun and they were all sitting round the table in the caravan.

'Only if we decide . . .' said Tim

guardedly. 'I mean, we were wrong yesterday, weren't we? The rest of us.'

'The rest of you might have been *right* yesterday,' said Ludo handsomely.

'Right, for the wrong reasons,' nodded Mini.

'What about the farmer, anyway?' asked Ben. 'Should we go and see him first?'

'He lives miles away,' Tim pointed out.

'What if the car's his?' wondered Amy.

'I'm sure it's not,' said Ludo. He picked up the club notebook and pencil. 'An empty barn. An empty house. A car in the barn. Signs of people in the house. It's too much of a coincidence. They've got to be connected.'

That's how they all felt. Now.

'We can forget about squatters,' said Mini. 'More likely thieves. They could have hired the car in London, or maybe they stole it. Come down here to pull off a big job somewhere. Found that The Nook's empty, so are holing up there for a few days . . .'

'Yes, that could be it,' said Tim excitedly.

'But how could they get *into* The Nook?' asked Amy, frowning. 'With new locks on the doors and everything.'

'Easy,' shrugged Ben, eager to get on

with the action. 'If they're professionals, they'll have skeleton keys and things. So you think it's back to Jermyn's, then, Tim? Not the farmer?'

'It's the house we promised Esme we'd protect,' said Amy with feeling. 'Not someone's silly old barn.'

Ludo's pencil was poised.

'I think it's got to be Jermyn's,' he said wryly. 'But we'll make a proper appointment this time. And let's get some hard information together. If there *is* a crook – or crooks – let's build up a sort of character profile. From the data we've got so far.'

'Great!' exclaimed Tim. 'A kind of photofit. Like the police do.'

'Well, they like black saloon cars,' said Ben.

'And strawberry jam,' said Tim.

'Very fond of carrots,' added Mini.

'Yes,' nodded Ludo. 'And raw ones at that. Wouldn't cook them, would they? Leaves too much mess.'

That reminded Amy: 'Extremely neat,' she suggested. 'Leave no obvious sign they're living in the house. I mean, wasn't the sitting-room tidy when we looked yesterday, Min?'

Ludo was writing it all down. 'And maybe like to have a nap in the afternoon?' he guessed.

'Why that?' asked Ben.

'Well – the shadow Esme thought she saw. It was Friday afternoon. But it was *upstairs* in one of the bedrooms. Anyway, I'll write it down with a question mark.'

'Do we all believe in Esme's shadow now?' asked Amy softly.

'Maybe,' said Ludo.

He passed the notebook round. Hands read it with satisfaction. It was impressive, somehow, to see it all written down in Ludo's firm handwriting:

INFORMATION FOR PHOTOFIT
1. Drives a saloon car.
2. Favourite car colour – black.
3. Likes strawberry jam.
4. Enjoys eating raw carrots.
5. Neat, methodical.
6. Takes a sleep in the afternoon?

Tim slid the radio phone to the centre of the table.

'Who's going to ring Jermyn's, then?' he asked tensely.

'I'll do it, if you like,' said Ludo, picking the phone up.

'Mr Jermyn's going to *have* to listen to us now, isn't he?' whispered Amy.

But it didn't turn out like that at all.

chapter 7

An Honorary Spout

*H*e didn't come in on Sundays, so there was no chance of seeing him. With or without an appointment, explained Ms Fender. Besides, if it were to do with The Nook again, Mr Jermyn would prefer her to deal with it. He didn't want to be bothered with them again.

Dee Fender, who had just the right name for the job, was in top form today. She was manning the telephone in the front office, defending and fobbing off for all she was worth.

She was also, as it turned out, extremely crushing.

'We've got important new information,' said Ludo down the telephone.

The other four pressed close to him, straining their ears to catch every syllable on the other end of the line.

'Oh? What?'

Ludo explained. Ms Fender listened in silence and then –

She laughed.

'Carrots? Kids have been stealing carrots, have they? Sure you didn't take some yourselves?'

'The light,' said Ludo firmly, keeping hold of his temper. 'And the jam.'

'Ah, yes. Well, it might interest you to know that Mr Jermyn showed some people over The Nook yesterday afternoon. The funny thing was, he didn't see a single squatter.'

Handles & Spouts exchanged slightly alarmed looks. Suddenly, they didn't feel quite so certain any more.

'But –' began Ludo.

'The light? Well, he'd switch on a different one before he left, wouldn't he? For security reasons. And rearrange the table, no doubt. Which reminds me, what were you doing near the kitchen window? You've been told not to trespass. If it happens once more, Mr Jermyn will have to report you all to Mr Kirk's sister.'

It wasn't an empty threat. There was an edge to her voice.

'Ring off, Ludo!' mouthed Tim in alarm. 'She's useless!'

'Sorry to have bothered you,' said Ludo quickly. ''Bye, then.'

'Phew!' exclaimed Ben. 'That's us squashed.'

'Can't have it getting back to Esme's Aunty Jan,' groaned Tim. 'That's the last thing she'd want!'

'We didn't even have time to tell her about the car in the barn,' said Amy in despair.

Ludo ran his fingers through his reddish fringe. It was all damp from the sweat of making the phone call.

'She'd only have said we were trespassing, going in the barn,' he sighed.

'Which we were, of course,' said Tim ruefully. He looked thoughtful. 'Question is, do we have a case, or don't we?'

They sat in silence for a while, frowning hard. The second conversation with Jermyn's had been almost as disconcerting as the first. Was it possible, again, that there were perfectly simple explanations for the things they'd seen?

'You're sure about the jam, Mini?' Tim asked at last. 'That some had gone?'

'Dead sure.'

'It's true someone could have just pinched the carrots,' said Amy uneasily, 'and Mr Jermyn could have put a different light on and maybe moved the jam pot around . . .'

'But he wouldn't have sat down and eaten some, would he?' protested Mini. 'Estate agents don't do things like that, when they're in the middle of trying to sell someone a house.'

'Maybe the people who were looking, maybe they had a kid with them,' said

Ben, thinking how much he liked strawberry jam himself.

'There was no sign of a spoon,' said Tim.

'And what about the car in the barn?' asked Amy.

'Even *that* could be innocent,' muttered Ben. 'Friends of the farmer or something.'

Ludo was staring at the list he'd made in the club notebook.

'So many little things,' he mused. 'You can take each of them in turn and explain them away. Starting with Esme's shadow which she's not even sure about herself. Only it doesn't feel right. Not one odd thing after another. Too much of a coincidence.'

'But we don't know, do we, Lu? What can we do about it?' said Tim. 'Where do we go from here?'

After the latest rebuff, they didn't feel brave enough to go and see the farmer, Mr Vincent. He was fearsome, always chasing people off his land. They would have to give away the fact that they'd been trespassing in his barn!

For the time being, they were stumped.

*

On Sunday evening, Amy went up to draw her curtains at the usual time.

As she gazed across the big dark field behind The Nook, she felt a tingle in the back of her neck.

The car headlights again! They were moving along behind the ragged hedge, on the far side of the field, dancing on the line of trees ahead.

'Tim!' she called.

Together they watched the mysterious lights disappear from view, over the hump of the far field.

'So there it goes again,' said Tim softly. 'The black car from London.'

'Tim, I've had an idea,' said Amy. 'Shall I invite Esme back after school tomorrow? Shall I ask Mum if she can stay the night? I mean, it *is* her mystery. She ought to be allowed to help, oughtn't she?'

'You mean, make her a sort of Honorary Spout for the night?' asked Tim.

'Yes! She might have some good ideas.'

'Well, why haven't we had any?' said Tim. 'If she can.'

'Look, don't you see? If we went back and kept watch on The Nook tomorrow evening, we wouldn't be trespassing any

more, would we? Not if Esme took us
there! I mean, it's her own garden. The
Nook still belongs to Esme and her dad.
So how would we be trespassing?'

'Brill, Amy!' exclaimed Tim.

'And I really do mean it, anyway, about
Esme being allowed to help.'

But Tim was already charging out of
the bedroom.

'I'll just go and ring the others and see
what they say!' he chortled.

'Essy! A friend on the phone!' called Aunty
Jan, coming upstairs and sounding pleased.

She looked into Esme's bedroom, and found her sitting on her beanbag, watching something on her new TV. But she didn't seem to be enjoying it very much. She looked rather red around the eyes.

Aunty Jan was beginning to wish that her brother wouldn't keep ringing Esme up. He'd rung again today. It must be costing him a fortune and it didn't really help.

'Mrs Dalladay's asked you back there for supper tomorrow, with Amy. And you can stay the night. Would you like that?'

'Stay the night with Amy?' Esme brightened up a bit. 'Yes, all right.'

A night in Back Lane, close to The Nook. Yes, she'd like that.

Amy and Esme then had a few words on the phone together. Amy had talked things over with Mini. They'd decided not to tell Esme anything. Not yet. They didn't want her sitting in Pelham St Cross, fretting. But there was something Amy wanted to do and it wouldn't be trespassing, if she asked first.

'I've got a whole lot of crumbs out of the bread-bin, Esme. Can I feed the birds for you, on the way to school?'

'That's just what I was planning!'

exclaimed Esme. 'I've got some crumbs, too. I'm going to nip along there and feed them, when I get off the bus.'

'Fine!' replied Amy. 'See you there, then.'

chapter 8

Something Else for the Photofit

*B*ut Amy was late on Monday morning and didn't see Esme at The Nook, after all. Handles & Spouts had been talking too much at the back door of the Knoll House. They hadn't noticed the time. They'd been talking enthusiastically about Esme being an Honorary Spout.

'Maybe tonight's the night we make our breakthrough!' exclaimed Ben.

'Does she know what it's about?' asked Ludo. 'That we've got suspicions?'

'No!' Amy shook her head. 'Didn't want her to fret all night.'

'Nor all day today, either.' Mini gave the Handles a warning look. 'Best not to say anything to her at school.'

'We weren't going to,' said Ben.

'Let's break it to her very gently, at club,' suggested Amy. 'After we've sworn her in as an Hon. Spout.'

'She'll feel good then, won't she?' nodded Tim. 'When she realizes she's got us five behind her and how hard we've been working on the case. She'll feel great when she sees that the Handles can handle things.'

'Not to mention the Spouts,' said Mini acidly.

After yesterday's setback, Tim's spirits were much revived.

Mini and Amy hurried along to school, behind the boys.

'Sure we've got time for that?' asked Mini worriedly, as Amy darted into The Nook's front garden, with the bag of crumbs. 'We're ever so late!'

'Won't take a sec! I'll just dump them on top of Esme's!' said Amy.

Running up the garden path, they could see that the birds were devouring the last of some crumbs on the bird-table.

'Here's a second helping for you!' laughed Amy, emptying the bag, as the birds watched from a safe distance. She would like to have hidden and seen them feed.

'OK!' said Mini. 'You've done it now. What are you waiting for? We've got to *hurry*!'

Second bell was ringing when they got to JVJ. They scrambled into hall only seconds before Mr Morton came striding in, to take assembly.

There was a tricky moment at dinner-time.

'Thanks for asking me back to your house, Amy!' said Esme shyly, as the three girls sat eating packed lunches. 'I've got my things!'

'Mum's going to put the chair-bed up in my room,' replied Amy.

'Can we go round to my house and see everything's all right?' asked Esme eagerly. 'Did you keep a look-out, over the weekend?'

'Go to your house, that's a good idea!' exclaimed Mini, hurriedly changing the subject.

'*Did* you see anything funny, your club?' pressed Esme.

For a moment they couldn't meet her eye. Then with great presence of mind, Mini clapped her hands.

'We've got something to tell you, Esme! About club,' she hissed.

'Club?' asked the fair-haired girl, looking worried.

Elizabeth Vine and Anna Patel, sitting further along the table, looked round with interest. They'd once asked if they could join.

'Sh!' said Mini importantly. She bent forward and whispered in Esme's ear.

'We're going to make you an honorary member! Just for tonight. The boys have agreed. OK?'

Esme looked pleased and nodded.

'I'd like that,' she said.

'We can all go and keep a look-out together,' Amy explained.

The awkward moment had passed.

In Arts & Crafts lesson that afternoon, Mini secretly made Esme a temporary membership badge. It had a little jug in the middle, just like theirs.

And after school that evening, in the Dalladays' yellow caravan, Esme Kirk was sworn in as an Honorary Spout.

They began to lay the ground.

'Everything the club does is secret,' Mini explained. 'So what we're going to tell you, we couldn't really discuss at school.'

'Besides, we didn't want you fretting about it,' said Amy.

'Could be nothing to it,' Ben added quickly, seeing Esme pale slightly. 'Could be a whole string of coincidences.'

'We've been accused of trespassing, you see. But now you're an Honorary Spout, you can take us along to The Nook!' said Tim eagerly. 'Anyway, six brains are better than five,' he added tactfully. 'If there *is* something going on, then tonight's the night we're going to solve it!'

'What *is* all this?' asked Esme, in alarm. Until a few moments ago, she'd been quite enjoying herself, drinking Coke and having her badge pinned on by Mini. 'So you *did* notice something over the weekend?'

Ludo was spokesperson.

He explained to Esme everything that had taken place, from the moment she'd asked them to keep an eye on The Nook for her.

She listened in silence, very pale, taking it all in.

Then Ludo handed her the club notebook, with the photofit details written down. She studied them carefully.

'Well, what do you think, Esme?' asked Amy softly.

'I think – well, first, I think you've all been really great,' she said humbly. She looked round at them, overcome with gratitude. 'I wasn't sure you understood. How I felt. Not really. And instead, you've been going to all this trouble.' She swallowed hard. 'Jermyn's sound awful. And to think I asked you to go there! It was really brave of you, to go and see them and ring them up and everything.'

That made them feel good. It made it all seem worthwhile.

'Amy means, what's your opinion?' prompted Ludo. He was blushing.

'Yes. Coming to that second. I don't know, to be honest.' Esme gave a little shiver. 'I just know I couldn't bear it if there *were* somebody in the house. It makes my skin crawl, even to think about it. I wish I could be sure about the shadow. Whether I saw it or not. I mean, Jermyn's wouldn't be able to explain *that* away, would they? But I *can't* be sure. The car's funny though, isn't it? I'm so pleased you've told me everything,' she said, closing the club notebook and handing it back to Ludo.

Then delayed reaction set in and she became agitated. She leapt up.

'But I'm not going to have someone eating Dad's carrots! They're ours! Cheek! I'm going to rush along there right now and have a look! I'll pretend I'm just feeding the birds!'

She was pulling a paper bag out of her pocket.

'Hey,' protested Ben. 'Not on your own, Es –'

'Calm down a bit, for goodness' sake!' said Tim.

'I'll just go as far as the bird-table, then. Get rid of these crumbs,' replied Esme tearfully.

Amy stared at the paper bag in surprise.

'Still got some left from this morning?' she asked.

'Didn't go this morning,' replied Esme. 'The bus was late so there wasn't time. Did you go, then?'

Amy and Mini exchanged astonished looks.

''Course!' said Amy. Her heart was going pit-a-pat. 'But we thought you'd just been –'

'*Someone had put some crumbs on the bird-table,*' explained Mini.

There was a startled silence.

It was broken by Ludo. His voice was tense.

'Well, that's something else for the photofit,' he said.

He wrote it down in the club notebook. They all looked at what he'd written:

7. Bird Lover.

It was too much. As Ludo said, it was just one thing too many.

Ben leaned across the table and touched Esme's arm.

'Sit down, Es,' he said. 'You're not going anywhere. Not on your own.'

She nodded and sat down. She looked very keyed-up. They all did.

'There's somebody there all right,' said Tim. 'There must be. Even Jermyn's can't explain this one away. Fresh breadcrumbs on the bird-table! First thing in the morning!'

'One funny thing too many,' repeated Ludo. 'This clinches it. There *are* people living in The Nook. Going out at night when darkness falls. In the black car. The one that's hidden in the barn.'

'Living in *our* house,' said Esme angrily. She sat stock still, but her mind was racing at great speed. 'Using *our house*, Dad's and mine. We've got to do something.'

'Yes, I think we should go into action,' said Ben glowering.

To everyone's surprise, Esme suddenly clasped her hands together.

'I know what we could do!' she whispered. 'I know the very thing! Oh, isn't it lucky there are six of us!'

chapter 9

Operation Barnstorm

'*I*t's getting dark early tonight!' puffed Tim, as the six of them cycled along the bridle-way. It was very bumpy. In the gloom, he'd gone straight over a tree root and nearly come off his bike.

'Lots of heavy cloud,' said Ben, glancing up. 'That's why.'

'Well, at least there won't be any moonlight, will there?' said Amy nervously. 'We mustn't be seen, must we!'

'No fear!' said Esme, who was riding Amy's red bike. Mrs Dalladay had lent Amy her nice old Raleigh.

Dusk was falling fast. It had still been quite light after supper, when they'd left the Knoll House.

'You'll be back before dark, won't you?' Mrs Dalladay had said.

'Don't worry, Mum. We've got lights,' Amy replied.

'If we're not, we'll be at The Nook,' Tim explained. 'Esme wants to poke around her old house, don't you, Es? So don't worry if we're a bit late, Mum!'

'All right,' nodded Mrs Dalladay. Good, she thought. Only just up the road. 'As long as I know where you are. You can have some hot chocolate when you get back.'

And they'd shot off to join up with the other three, who were waiting for them on the corner of Letcombe Lane.

The journey that had taken ages with Harry took less than half an hour on the speeding bikes. Ahead, along the bridle-way, the black silhouettes of the trees came in sight. They knew from yesterday that the barn lay not far beyond. It was now hidden in the gathering darkness.

'I think we're only just going to make it!' panted Mini, pumping along on her small-wheeled shopper. 'By the time we've found somewhere good to dump the bikes and get ourselves into position, it'll be nearly pitch black!'

'And that's the time the car leaves the barn, isn't it?' said Amy.

They all looked rather pale and tense, especially Esme.

At the end of the line of trees, they dismounted.

'Let's shove all the bikes in here,' suggested Ben. 'Behind those two trees.'

They left them there and continued on foot. They moved stealthily now, hugging the ragged hedge that would bring them to the wide gap by the old timber barn. Tim led the way, using the front lamp off his bicycle as a torch.

'Operation Barnstorm!' he whispered.

That was the code name they'd given their plan.

They reached the gap in the hedge, then pulled back, still safely under cover. Their eyes were fixed on the barn's big double doors.

The doors were firmly shut.

'We're in time, then,' said Ludo, in relief. 'They haven't come to get the car yet!'

'They'd have passed us, if they had!' pointed out Amy. She gave a little shiver.

It was getting blacker by the minute. Soon, they couldn't see the barn at all.

'You're sure there's no way out of the barn, Es, once someone's locked it?' whispered Ben, licking dry lips. 'No windows at the back, no gaps anywhere?'

'Positive!' breathed Esme. 'I should know, shouldn't I?'

She'd told them all about it. How once, when she was little, she'd fallen asleep behind some hay-bales in there. Mr Vincent had come and shut the doors, not realizing! She'd had to hammer and shout for nearly an hour before Mum and Dad came and found her.

That was what had given her the idea.

'We'd better stop talking now,' warned Tim. He extinguished his cycle lamp. 'Everybody OK? When they go into the barn, we charge! Handles take the left door, Spouts take the right. Got it? The minute we hear them unlock the car doors and get in, we move like lightning!'

'Yep! We've got to get those barn doors shut in about five seconds flat!' said Ben excitedly.

They knew the plan off by heart.

Now all they had to do was wait.

They crouched behind the hedge in total silence and total blackness.

'They're late,' thought Amy. She

glanced over her shoulder, nervously. Supposing they didn't come from the house at all? Supposing they came from this direction, along the bridle-way?

They were banking on the theory that the car and house mysteries were connected. But were they?

Mini was thinking the same thing. She heard a rustling sound in the hedge, not far behind her. It made her jump. But it must have been a bird. Somewhere, an owl hooted.

It was a strain for all of them, crouched down like statues in one position with their ears attuned for the slightest sound. At any moment they expected to hear voices, coming across the field from the direction of The Nook. But there was nothing.

Perhaps we're too late, thought Tim to himself, aching with suspense. We know they fed the birds this morning. We know they've taken the car out three nights running. But maybe not tonight! Maybe they've gone. We don't even know there's a car *in* the barn any longer.

Then, from the far side of the field, came a faint, eerie sound.

Esme clutched Amy's arm so tight that it hurt.

'That's our back door!' she hissed. 'It always creaks like that.'

Then they all heard a muffled little thud. The sound of a door being shut.

'Sh!' warned Tim.

So they'd come out of The Nook. They'd come out of the back door and closed it behind them. Right now, they'd be climbing over the old trodden-down fence, stepping into the farmer's field. How long would it take them to cross the field? Three minutes? Two?

And then they'd be here.

In the darkness, Handles & Spouts huddled closer together, waiting and listening. None of them would have admitted to the sudden fear they felt. They wanted to turn and flee. But they couldn't run away, not now.

This was it, then. Operation Barnstorm.

Those last three minutes were the worst. Waiting and listening. The silence was eerie. They were coming across the field without speaking! Perhaps it was only one person?

The soft stubble muffled any sound of approaching footsteps.

But suddenly –

A beam of torchlight played across the
barn doors.

So they'd arrived! A little later than
usual, but they were here. They'd come
once again to collect the black saloon car
and drive it out of the barn.

As the six of them crouched behind the
hedge, they could see nothing except that
beam of torchlight, close, brighter,
alighting briefly on the doors' heavy
latches.

Then came the sound of the latches
being lifted and the further door being
pulled back, to the accompaniment of

93

grunting sounds. It was hard work for one person. They were sure now that it was only one person. After a pause and some heavy breathing, there came a grating sound as the nearer of the two heavy doors was pulled open.

They heard more movements and the rattle of keys as the person went inside the barn and they saw a figure silhouetted for a moment. At long last came the sound they'd been waiting for:

Click!

The car door was being unlocked. The person would now be climbing into it!

'Charge!' hissed Tim.

With Tim's lamp to guide them, they moved silently and at great speed through the gap in the hedge and along the short track. They could see that the two great doors were wide open now. Inside the barn was only blackness.

Then they dived behind the doors, boys to the left, girls to the right.

'Heave!' said Tim.

With three on each side, it was easy. It took no more than a few moments.

As the doors met in the middle, there came a cry from inside the barn, the sound of the car engine and a dazzling shaft of brilliance as its headlights shot through the gap beneath the closed doors.

But they were already dropping the heavy latches into place.

'Got you!' yelled Ben, in wild triumph.

'Run!' shouted Tim. 'Through The Nook!'

'The police!' echoed Ludo.

Tim turned the beam of his lamp on to the bumpy field and they started to run. They had it all planned. They'd take the quickest route to the Knoll House and ring the police from there. Collecting their bikes could wait.

They all ignored the furious hammering on the doors behind them and the angry voice crying, '*Let me out of here!* LET ME OUT!'

All of them, that is, except Esme.

chapter 10

Sunny Day at JVJ

Mini heard Esme give a little cry behind her in the blackness and ploughed on fast, trying to catch up with Tim's bobbing light ahead.

'Wait for me and Esme!' she shouted crossly. 'We can't see, you nut!'

'Sorry!' gasped Tim, pulling up until Mini came abreast. 'Just scared he'll escape before we ring the police!'

'Where's Esme?' asked Ludo in alarm. 'Isn't she with you, Min?'

She wasn't. They all turned and looked back, peering through the blackness.

'Where is she?' asked Amy.

'There. I bet she fell over or something!' exclaimed Mini.

'Come on, Tim,' said Ben tersely. 'Let's go back and find her.'

They retraced their steps.

'She's disappeared!' whispered Mini, in surprise.

They were almost back at the barn before they saw her. They saw her feet, first.

It was an astonishing sight. Esme was standing by the barn doors, her back to them. Her feet were illuminated in the shaft of car headlights that seeped out from under the locked doors. Her face was pressed against the doors and she seemed to be talking to the person inside.

'What on earth does she think she's doing?' gasped Amy.

'Es! Come back *here*!' shouted Ben.

They started to close in on her. The car's engine was still ticking. They could hear the man's voice.

'Open up, then. There's a good girl.'

Like somebody in a trance, Esme lifted the two big latches. Then she tugged feverishly at one of the doors, to make an opening, while the man pushed at the other from the inside. The other five stood there, frozen with panic.

'*Esme!*' bellowed Tim, recovering his wits.

But now the doors were open and a figure stepped through. The scene was bathed in the brilliant twin spotlights of the car's beams, like a tableau.

He was a short, cheery sort of man. He was holding his arms wide. Esme hurled herself into his arms and started to cry with happiness.

'Dad!' she sobbed. 'You've come back home!' She said it several times.

'Don't cry, Essy.' He was holding her close.

'I just knew it was your voice, Dad! You've come back!'

Mr Kirk cradled his daughter's head against his shoulder.

'Never went, love,' he grunted. 'Never went in the first place.'

Handles & Spouts, witnessing this astonishing scene, gasped amongst themselves. Amy felt a big, emotional lump coming up into her throat.

And now Esme was saying, 'Please don't sell The Nook, Dad. Please don't go away.'

'You want us to be together, Essy? You really do, then?' He sounded so pleased and happy. 'I only wanted to make some money, Essy. I never wanted to leave

Jugminster. It was all for you, girl. I wanted you to have all the nice things I couldn't give you if we stayed together.'

'I don't want nice things,' replied Esme. 'I just want my dad back.'

It had been the hardest decision of Mr Kirk's life, to accept the job he'd been offered in New Zealand. It was also an unselfish one. Working on an isolated dairy farm, fifty miles from the nearest town, did not appeal to him, however well paid. Leaving Esme and leaving The Nook, with all its happy memories of his wife, had appealed even less.

But Mr Kirk had convinced himself that it was right for Esme's sake. His wife's wages had helped to pay the mortgage on The Nook. Ever since she'd died, life had been quite a struggle. He dreaded the thought that, as Esme got older, he wouldn't be able to give her the nice clothes and holidays and school trips that other youngsters had. Jan and Roger would be good to her and with the money he could send from New Zealand, she'd never want for anything.

He'd put a brave face on it, going to New Zealand. Esme hadn't seemed to mind too much. Until the day she'd waved him off on the coach to London Airport. The expression on her face that morning had filled him with wretchedness.

She'd get over it, surely? She'd soon adjust to her new life, wouldn't she, and settle down nicely with Jan and Roger?

Or was he making a dreadful mistake, one he'd regret for the rest of his life?

Suddenly, Mr Kirk knew that he had to make sure.

He wasn't due to start his new job for another three weeks. He'd been planning to see something of New Zealand first, a beautiful country by all accounts. Well, he'd forgo that. He'd change his ticket and spend another couple of weeks in England.

But it would have to be a secret. The only way he could tell for sure whether Esme was settling down or not was if she *thought* he were in New Zealand. He'd phone her a few times and pretend that's where he was.

He couldn't afford a hotel, that was for sure. But how about The Nook? He'd kept a set of keys, for sentiment. Mr Jermyn had told him there wouldn't be many viewers. The property market was very slow at present – Jermyn's were having to open seven days a week, to try and drum up business! He'd need some transport, of course. He'd sold his car.

So Mr Kirk had changed his ticket at London Airport, hired a car for two weeks (black, like his old one), then turned round and driven straight back to Jugminster.

Of course, he wouldn't be able to park the car in Back Lane, as usual. But that didn't matter.

He knew just the place to keep it hidden!

'Dad had to do all his living after dark,' Esme explained to Handles & Spouts. 'He drove to transport cafés and places to get hot meals and then walked for miles. He could tell I wasn't settling down. He'd walk and walk, turning it all over in his mind. He kept thinking he'd make one more phone call before coming to a decision.'

'So he just used the house during the daytime, snatching a bit of sleep?' said Ben.

'Yes, but he's used to that. Keeping funny hours. Staying up at night delivering calves, that sort of thing,' explained Esme. 'He's a light sleeper. He saw me in the

102

garden that afternoon – and he heard you come in, both times. His worst moment was when Mr Jermyn brought those people to view the house!' She smiled. 'He dived out the back door and locked himself in the outside loo!'

'Lucky they didn't want to inspect it!' said Mini.

They all laughed.

It was a sunny day at JVJ. It was the dinner hour and they'd taken Esme to the far side of the playing-field, down to the bank of the stream. They'd wanted to talk to her and make sure she was all right because this morning she'd seen her father off on the coach to the airport again.

He'd agreed to go to New Zealand for just six months, to help his new boss through a staff crisis. He'd have to work very long hours. But he'd earn enough to pay back his air fare and bring money home to England as well.

'And Jermyn's have managed to let the house for six months,' Esme told them. 'Isn't it good? It's going to cover all the mortgage payments while Dad's away!'

She looked very serene.

'And you don't mind, any more?' asked Amy cautiously. 'The idea of strangers being in the house and touching your furniture and stuff?'

'Not a bit,' said Esme. 'I was muddled, you see. It wasn't the house and furniture I was missing. It was Dad. I've got something to look forward to now, haven't I? We'll start again. I know we'll manage somehow. And when I'm older I'll be able to do jobs like baby-sitting and stuff and help pay for things.'

As they all trooped back across the field for lessons, Tim quite suddenly threw his arm round Esme's shoulders.

'And when you grow up you can be a detective, Es,' he said. 'You'd be good. You were great as an Honorary Spout!'

'The best!' agreed Amy. Esme had solved the mystery herself! She'd solved it in one evening.

'I'd be useless!' protested Esme. She turned to Ludo. 'Shall I tell you something? That photofit you built up: favourite car colour, black; likes raw carrots; loves strawberry jam; tidy and methodical; likes sleeping in the afternoon; bird lover.'

'Yes?' asked Ludo eagerly.

'Well, that's my dad. That's him to a T. You all got every detail right. It was

staring me in the face and I couldn't see it.'

Ludo grinned. As he walked, he was definitely swaggering a bit.

'We can be quite brilliant at times,' he said.

Mr Jermyn was impressed, too. The big box of chocolates he sent round to them was delicious. Even Ms Fender had signed the card.

In the same series

BOYS V. GIRLS AT JUG VALLEY JUNIORS

When Peter Pay's bike vanishes from Jug Valley Juniors, Tim Dalladay and his friends form the Handles and promise to track down the thief. 'This isn't girls' stuff,' they tell Tim's twin sister, Amy, and her best friend. 'It needs boys to handle it.'

As a joke the girls call themselves the Spouts, but the disappearance of Mrs Dalladay's bike from outside Tesco in broad daylight gives them a serious quest of their own.

And so the junior school detectives go into action – mostly against each other. Yet they should be working together if they want to avoid danger.

THE HEADMASTER'S GHOST AT JUG VALLEY JUNIORS

Tim, Amy and the rest of Handles & Spouts can't believe that Mr Morton, the headmaster of Jug Valley Juniors, would have shouted and thrown biscuits at some of the parents at the open evening. He's always been popular and respected. Now, despite his claim that he hadn't even been there, he could face the sack.

Could it have been a ghost everyone saw that evening? A poltergeist? Handles & Spouts are determined to find out in the second exciting story of this thrilling series.

HANDS UP! AT JUG VALLEY JUNIORS

Ben couldn't guess the trouble he would cause when he accidentally kicks Charlie Smith's old football into the rector's garden.

When Ben and his friends in Handles & Spouts search the garden after school, there's no sign of the ball. They get Charlie a new ball, but Charlie is desperate to find the old one.

Who can have taken the old ball, and why does Charlie want it back so badly? Handles & Spouts have some surprises in store in this third story of a fantastic new series.

Also by Anne Digby

'Far better than the run-of-the-mill adventure story' – *The Good Book Guide to Children's Books*

ME, JILL ROBINSON AND THE TELEVISION QUIZ

Moving to Haven is full of unexpected excitements for the Robinson family. But for Jill, making friends with the high-spirited daughter of the town's mayor makes it all worth while.

However, Melinda isn't everyone's favourite person, least of all her father's. So when she gets the chance to compete in a television quiz, she really hopes that at last he will be proud of her. But it isn't that simple.

ME, JILL ROBINSON AND THE SEASIDE MYSTERY

Keeping an eye on her younger brother Tony certainly makes the Robinsons' seaside holiday an exciting one for Jill. Why does he keep disappearing on his own, and who is his new friend, Sam? Dad gets more and more angry with Tony, so Jill and her best friend Lindy try to solve the mystery, only to find themselves in real trouble!

ME, JILL ROBINSON AND THE CHRISTMAS PANTOMIME

Jill's sister, Sarah, is helping Roy Brewster produce the Youth Club's Christmas panto and Jill is dying for a leading role. It looks set to be great fun for Jill and Lindy, until the Runcorn boys get involved and spoil it for everyone. But Jill discovers that their leader, Big Harry, isn't as tough as he makes out.

ME, JILL ROBINSON AND THE
SCHOOL CAMP ADVENTURE

When Jill and Lindy start looking after a stray dog at the school camp on a remote Scottish island, the scheming Rita is determined to get them into trouble and Miss Rawlings threatens to take Cu away from them. But when Rita goes missing on the mysterious island it is only Cu who can find her.

ME, JILL ROBINSON AND THE
PERDOU PAINTING

Jill is really excited when Polly Pudham invites her home for tea because 'Pud' lives in the most expensive road in Haven. But why is Jill so interested in the painting Polly's father has just bought? And what happens when Jill's sister goes to the Pudhams' cocktail party to see the painting – what is she *supposed* to have done?

ME, JILL ROBINSON AND THE
STEPPING STONES MYSTERY

Feelings in Haven Youth Club run high when it is decided how to spend its hard-earned money. Not everyone is in favour of Roy Brewster's cracking idea to transform the river at the stepping stones bend . . . Then the bridge-building project is sabotaged! But who could have done it? Sir Harry, the local landowner, Jill's brother, Tony, or perhaps someone from the club? Jill and Lindy are determined to find out.

By Alan Davidson

A FRIEND LIKE ANNABEL

Thirteen-year-old Annabel Fidelity Bunce is the wonder of Addendon – adored by her best friend Kate, considered by many of her fellow pupils in 3G at Lord Willoughby's School to be off her head and warily tolerated by teachers and other adults of the town. These riotously funny stories prove that with a friend like Annabel life is certainly never dull.

JUST LIKE ANNABEL

Taking sides with a bored donkey against Mrs da Susa and Mrs Stringer, pillars of Addendon, Annabel and Kate are soon on the trail of the Franks–Walters enigma.

EVEN MORE LIKE ANNABEL

'There'll be a reign of terror,' Annabel predicts when the repellent Julia Channing is appointed Monitor of the Band Room (the school's Junior Leisure and Recreation Centre).

THE NEW, THINKING ANNABEL

In these three stories Annabel, in her inimitable manner, struggles to apply some thought to her actions.

LITTLE YEARNINGS OF ANNABEL

What's the reason, Kate wonders, for Annabel's desperate desire to get into the Guinness Book of Records? Is it really because of what Auntie Lucy Loxby said about Mozart?

'Sparkling Annabel comedies' – *Guardian*
'Hilarious . . . really good fun' – BBC Radio
'Annabel books are infectious fun' – *Birmingham Post*
'Davidson has a style which grows on you – as all good styles should – and which undoubtedly accounts for the popularity of these stories' – *Times Educational Supplement*